Good Luck,
Louisa

A RED FOX BALLET BOOK

First published in Great Britain by Red Fox,
an imprint of Random House Children's Books

This edition published 2002

1 3 5 7 9 10 8 6 4 2

Copyright © Adèle Geras, 2002
Illustrations copyright © Karen Popham, 2002

The rights of Adèle Geras and Karen Popham to be identified as the author
and illustrator of this work has been asserted in accordance with the Copyright,
Designs and Patents Act 1988

Red Fox Books are published by Random House Children's Books,
61-63 Uxbridge Road, London W5 5SA,
a division of The Random House Group Ltd,
in Australia by Random House Australia (Pty) Ltd,
20 Alfred Street, Milsons Point, Sydney, NSW 2061, Australia,
in New Zealand by Random House New Zealand Ltd,
18 Poland Road, Glenfield, Auckland 10, New Zealand,
and in South Africa by Random House (Pty) Ltd,
Endulini, 5A Jubilee Road, Parktown 2193, South Africa

THE RANDOM HOUSE GROUP Limited Reg. No. 954009
www.randomhouse.co.uk

A CIP catalogue record for this book is available from the British Library.

ISBN 0 09 940944 5

Printed and bound in Great Britain by Bookmarque Ltd, Croydon, Surrey

RED FOX BALLET BOOKS

Good Luck, Louisa

by Adèle Geras

illustrated by Karen Popham

RED FOX

Chapter One

Mrs Posnansky is in hospital. She's our neighbour, and I like her fourth best in the whole world, after Mum, Dad and my sister, Annie. Sometimes, when I'm cross with Annie, I like Mrs Posnansky third best. She's Russian and she's interested in ballet because her mother used to be a dancer long ago. She knows how much I want to be a ballerina and ever since I started she's always done everything she possibly could to help me. When I was one of the Little Swans in the dancing display last year, she gave me the feathered headband her mother wore when she was in *Swan Lake* and it's my lucky mascot now, and lives in my special box of treasures.

When I heard that she was ill, I was really sad. We've been to visit her a lot and even though it is horrible seeing her in her bed, looking all small and wrinkled, and with her hair down round her shoulders, I never tell her that, and she says I really cheer her up with my stories about what's happening in my ballet class.

Yesterday, though, Mum told Annie and me some good news when we got back from school. Mrs Posnansky was well enough to come home.

"When'll she be here?" I asked. "I'm planning something really special to welcome her."

"I'm going to fetch her on Monday, next week."

"And it's Thursday today." I said. "We haven't got much time. I must phone Phoebe and Tony straight away. Is that all right?"

"Can't you wait till tomorrow?" Mum said, sighing. She often sighs when she's speaking to me. "You'll see them both at school, won't you?"

"I need to tell them what's happening. They'll both have to come here at the weekend for rehearsals . . . that'll be OK, won't it?"

"I suppose so. Go on and phone them then," Mum said, and went into the kitchen.

"Rehearsals for what?" said Annie after she'd gone.

"A Welcome Home ballet for Mrs Posnansky," I told her. "I've been thinking about it for ages. Well, for a day or two. And I've already asked Phoebe and Tony and they say they'll do it with me. Only I thought we'd have a while to practise and now we've only got a couple of days."

"I thought you'd be happy that Mrs Posnansky's so much better," said Annie.

"Of course I'm happy," I said. "But it means we haven't got much time. And I need you, too, Annie. Will you help me?"

"As long as you don't want me to dance," Annie said, and I laughed. It was hard to imagine my sister dancing, but she is very good at drawing and painting and designing things. Dad says she's the artistic one in our family.

"No," I said, "you don't have to dance. What I'd like you to do is make a huge banner with 'Welcome Home, Mrs Posnansky' painted on it and you can decorate it as much as you like. Will you do that?"

"I suppose so . . . I don't know about huge, though. Where am I going to get a huge bit of paper?"

"Maybe you could stick lots of little bits of paper together or something?" I said.

"You don't need to do that," said Mum. I didn't realise she was still listening. She smiled and said, "I'll give Annie a white sheet, one of our old ones, and she can paint on that. That'd be big enough wouldn't it, Weezer?"

"Louisa," I said. My family were *useless* at getting my name right. Weezer was what they used to call me before I decided to become a dancer, but they kept forgetting that I wanted to be called Louisa now. "A sheet would be brilliant. Thanks, Mum. I'm going to phone Phoebe and Tony."

Phoebe and Tony are my best friends. They both love dancing but Tony has started grumbling about it a bit. He moans about having to get up early on Saturday mornings for our Special Advanced Class, and on Tuesdays when we go to ballet after school he says he'd rather play on his computer. I take no notice and I make him come with me, however much he grumbles, and he always enjoys himself in the end. When I first told him about the Welcome Home ballet that I was going to make up for Mrs Posnansky, he didn't really want to be in it at all.

"But I need you!" I said. "You can't have a proper ballet without a boy. It wouldn't look right. I need you to be the Prince."

"Why don't you do a dance without a prince?" Tony asked. "You and Phoebe could do that Bluebell Dance you did in class the other day."

"No, Tony," I said. "I've got it all worked out. We're going to do a bit from *Sleeping Beauty*. Mrs Posnansky loves that story. It's her favourite. I'm going to be Sleeping Beauty and you can come and find me and wake me with a kiss."

Tony made a stupid face, but I took no notice. Boys are just silly when it comes to kissing.

"Can I be the Lilac Fairy?" Phoebe asked. "My mum has a gorgeous mauve scarf I could wear."

I nodded. Phoebe would make a lovely Lilac Fairy. I had thought about the steps we'd all have to do and I'd even found a bit on my *Sleeping Beauty* tape which our dance could fit into. I'd been planning Mrs Posnansky's treat for a couple of days and now that I knew when she was leaving hospital, I had to act quickly and start rehearsals. I dialled Phoebe's number first.

"Phoebe? It's me . . . Louisa. Can you come to my house on Saturday, after ballet? Only Mrs Posnansky is getting home on Monday evening and . . . yes, that's right. *Sleeping Beauty*. You haven't forgotten, have you? . . . Oh, goody! See you at school tomorrow, then. We can talk about it some more during break. . . . Right. Bye!"

Then I phoned Tony, which felt a bit funny because he lives next door and I usually go and see him when I want to tell him something.

"It's me," I said. "I can't come round because I've got to do some planning."

When I told him about the rehearsal on Saturday, he started to give me all sorts of reasons why he couldn't come, but I knew he was just making excuses, as usual.

"Stop it, Tony!" I said. "You promised! I need you to be the Prince. I've told you and told you. And I'm not having my Welcome Home ballet spoiled because of you, so there!"

He gave in in the end. He always does. I went to find Annie. She was upstairs in our bedroom doing her homework.

"It's going to be fantastic, Annie!" I said. "Mrs Posnansky will be thrilled to bits!"

Chapter Two

By the time Mrs Posnansky arrived on Monday, Phoebe, Tony and I were all ready for our performance. The Welcome Home sheet was hanging on the wall beside the front door. I told Annie and my mum that it had to go there.

"I want Mrs Posnansky to see it as soon as she gets out of the car," I said. Mum and Annie and Tony's dad on his ladder all agreed; and we nailed it up so that the lovely pictures and letters could be seen from a long way away.

"It's brilliant," Tony said, looking at it carefully. "I like those little dancers round the edge."

"Thanks," said Annie.

Mum was looking after Mrs Posnansky's

keys, so she opened the house for us and Tony and I went in to get our stage prepared. Then Phoebe arrived carrying her ballet case, and we all looked at the space we were going to have to dance in. Mum and I rolled the carpet back and put the sofa in just the right spot for me to lie on while I was being Sleeping Beauty.

"That's OK, isn't it?" I asked Phoebe. "I'll put the tape recorder here on the sideboard. There'll be room for your steps, won't there?"

Phoebe nodded. I showed her the curtain she had to hide behind while she was waiting to come on and after she'd finished dancing, and then Tony wanted to know where he was coming in from so we sorted that out, and then it was time to get dressed.

"We'll go back home to do that," I told them. "It wouldn't feel right to go upstairs in Mrs Posnansky's house."

We went back to my bedroom, and changed into our ballet costumes.

Phoebe looked really pretty in her tutu with the mauve scarf round her hair and hanging down her back. Tony was wearing black tights and a satin shirt which really belonged to his mother but which made him look very royal.

"I feel stupid," he said when I told him that, but I said, "You look exactly like a prince, so stop grumbling."

I'd borrowed a dress from Miss Matting's costume cupboard. It had a lovely long skirt and there were tiny satin roses stitched to the straps. When I danced, it floated round my legs. I thought it was beautiful.

"It doesn't look much like a nightie," Tony said. "Isn't Sleeping Beauty supposed to be asleep?"

Phoebe and I both laughed.

"It's not meant to be a nightie, silly!" I told him. "You've forgotten . . . Sleeping Beauty falls asleep during her sixteenth birthday party. It's a party dress, so there! And she's called Princess Aurora in the ballet."

We hid in the dining-room while Mum and Annie opened the door for Mrs Posnansky. She was really pleased with the Welcome Home sheet. I could hear her saying so as she went into the lounge.

"Is a wonderful surprise! I am so happy to be in my house," she said. "You are so kind to come to greet me. So kind. I will sit now, yes."

"What's your mum saying?" Tony asked. Now that they'd all gone into the lounge, I couldn't hear what they were saying very clearly.

"Shh!" I said. "I'm trying to hear."

"Where is my ballerina?" Mrs Posnansky said. "Where is Louisa?" Then I heard Annie say what we'd decided she should say.

"She's waiting with her friends to do a special dance that she's made up just to show you how happy she is that you're home. Sit back and watch carefully."

Mrs Posnanksy started clapping and cried, "Such a surprise! So beautiful! A dance for me . . . how I am moved!"

As soon as the music began, I went into the lounge and lay on the sofa, pretending to be asleep. Phoebe came in too and, once I was lying quite still, she began to dance. Mrs Posnansky and Mum and Annie sat on the chairs I'd put near the bay window and watched while she twirled and spun. Her mauve scarf really did look just like fairy wings. I know I was supposed to be asleep, but I can look as though my eyes are closed and still see what's going on. I just sort of nearly close them, but don't really.

I was worried in case Tony forgot to

come in, but he was right on his cue. He and Phoebe did the bit of the dance where she showed him the way to Princess Aurora's room. Then he pretended he was cutting through the hedge of roses with his sword. Then he bent over and kissed me on the forehead. I was longing to get up and start dancing, so it was quite hard to wake up slowly, which is what I had to do to fit into the music.

Once I was up, though, I started to dance the steps that I'd been practising for days. It was supposed to show how happy Princess Aurora was to be awake at last. I stretched out my arms and pretended to yawn. Then I did a lot of jetés and pirouettes, and Tony was supposed to be watching me and feeling happy too. Then we danced together for a while. Tony helped me do some quite hard arabesques and Phoebe stood by the wall, looking at us. Then, at the end, we all bowed in front of Mrs Posnansky. When I looked up from my curtsey, I saw that she was crying.

"You're not supposed to cry!" I said. "We did it because we wanted you to be happy, not sad!"

"These are the happiness tears, darling Louisa. I so admire this dance. Is so wonderful. You are such good dancers, all of you. And Louisa, you are the choreographer, too? Wonderful! Superb! Oh, you must come here for me to give you big kisses."

Mrs Posnansky smelled powdery and sweet as she kissed me and she felt very thin when I put my arms round her. She whispered to me as she held me and what she said was, "You are beautiful dancer, my Little Swan. Beautiful!"

I felt so happy that I almost burst.

Chapter Three

$\mathcal{J}$t was good to have Mrs Posnansky back, but my happiness didn't last very long. The very next Tuesday at ballet, Miss Matting had some bad news for us all.

"Sit down, children," she said to us at the end of our lesson. "I have something I want to tell you."

"What can it be?" Phoebe whispered to me.

"I don't know," I said. "But she's been looking dead sad all through the lesson, hasn't she? Did you notice?"

"I did," said Tony. "I bet she's going to say she's leaving and we'll have to have another teacher."

"That'll be awful!" I said. "I really like Miss Matting."

"You'll probably like the new teacher," said Tony.

"You don't know it's going to be about Miss Matting leaving," I said. "Do you?"

"Shh!" said Phoebe. "She's going to say something."

Miss Matting stood at the front of the hall and looked at the floor.

"This is a very sad day for me," she said. "And I expect a lot of you will be very sad too. I'll tell you as quickly as I can, because it's best to get bad news over quickly, I think. My ballet school is closing. I'm afraid that

I'm leaving the area, and I haven't been able to find anyone to take charge of my pupils, so I'm going to have to close the school altogether. There are some other classes in town, of course, and I can give you details of those, but you'll only be able to come here till the end of the month. I'm very sorry indeed. Truly. But I know that at least some of you will continue learning with someone else and go on to do great things. Next week I'll put up a list with details on it of all the other ballet classes. Try not to be too sad, children. Goodnight, everyone."

Nobody said anything. We just stood up and went to get changed in silence. I felt as though everything had suddenly gone very dark. When we were all in our street clothes, we went outside to wait for Phoebe's mum to pick us up.

"That's it, then," said Tony. "I'm giving up ballet. I'm going to do gym classes instead. They do them at the Sports Centre on Wednesday nights."

"You can't!" I said. "You're so good, Tony. They always need good boys at ballet school. Oh, please don't stop doing ballet. You can come to another class. I'm going to find one. I can't not do ballet, I just can't. And you're like me, aren't you, Phoebe?"

Phoebe shook her head. She said, "But I know what Miss Matting's going to say. My mum looked into all the classes around here when we moved, and they're really not very good. The only decent place is the Sheridan Academy, but it's right on the other side of town, and anyway, they don't just let anyone go. You have to audition, and they only take a few people every year. We'll never get in." She sounded really gloomy.

"We've got to try though, Phoebe. Haven't we? Don't you think we're good enough?" I said.

"I don't know," said Phoebe. "I don't know how good the other people are who want to go there. They might be much better."

"Miss Matting will know," I said, trying to cheer myself up a bit. "She'll know if we have any chance at all of getting in. Let's ask her next week."

"Ask me what, dears?" said Miss Matting, who had just locked up and was now standing behind us.

We gathered round her. I said, "Oh, Miss Matting, I'm so glad you're still here. Phoebe's mum is coming to get us, but she hasn't arrived yet. Can we ask you something?"

"Of course, Louisa. I hope I can give you an answer."

"It's about the Sheridan Academy," Phoebe said. "Do you think we're good enough to audition to get in there?"

"Certainly you're good enough," said Miss Matting. "But I should warn you that the auditions are very competitive and even if you do get in, there's always the cost to consider. I believe the fees are very high indeed. But that shouldn't stop you from trying. The auditions are two weeks away, so you won't have too long to wait."

Phoebe's mum's car drew up beside us.

"Thank you, Miss Matting," I said, trying to sound normal. But I felt like bursting into tears. What if Mum and Dad couldn't afford the fees for the Sheridan Academy? What would happen then? How could I become a ballet dancer now? Whatever was I going to do?

As soon as I got home, I ran up to our bedroom to find Annie. She's good at knowing the best thing to do, when you've got a problem. She listened to me while I told her everything, and then she said,

"I think you'd better ask Mum. Or Dad. Maybe he could find the money, if it was really important. You don't know exactly how much they are, do you? And in any case, shouldn't you do the audition first? If you don't get in, then all the worry about the money would have been for nothing."

I picked up my pillow and threw it at her head.

"You're horrible!" I shouted. "How can you say I won't get in? Don't you think I'm a good dancer? That's such a nasty thing to say. I can't believe you said it. I'm not talking to you, ever again, till you take it back."

I lay flat on the bed, and tears slid down my face and made my neck wet.

Annie threw the pillow back at me, and I grabbed it and pulled it over my head. It didn't stop me hearing what she said.

"You're being silly, you really are. I didn't mean you're not a good dancer. You're ever so good and you know you are. But you don't know how good everyone else is who's going to audition, do you? So you may not get in. You'd better start thinking about that, or you're going to be dead upset when it happens, aren't you?"

I sniffed a bit under my pillow. Annie was right. She usually was. I felt worse than ever. But I had to be able to dance, I just had to. What would I do if I didn't get in? Where else could I go to learn to be a ballet dancer?

Chapter Four

For the next two weeks, Phoebe and I did nothing but practise and practise for our audition at the Sheridan Academy.

"We don't really know, do we, what we'll be asked to do," said Phoebe.

"Miss Matting thought we should prepare a little solo each. And she said they'll probably have a sort of class where they can look at everyone together . . . everyone who's auditioning."

We decided to go over all the things we did in class every week and to help one another with our dances. We were going to do the ones I'd made up for Mrs Posnansky's Welcome Home and we rehearsed them and rehearsed them until we could probably have danced them perfectly in our sleep.

When we weren't practising, we talked about the audition, and by the time the actual day arrived, Mum and Annie and Mrs Posnansky were all sick and tired of hearing about it. One of the things we kept talking about was whether we could afford my fees if I did get in. Mum said, "I'll just repeat what I said at the very beginning of all this: go and see what they say about you, Louisa, and we'll worry about the fees if you're accepted."

I didn't say anything. I was going to try my very hardest, but it was difficult to stop worrying about whether or not I was going to be good enough.

On the day we had to go to the Sheridan Academy, Phoebe's mum gave me and Tony a lift in their car.

"I'm not nervous at all," said Tony. "If I don't get in, I'll do gymnastics. I think I'd like that better than ballet anyway."

"You don't mean it!" Phoebe and I said together. We couldn't imagine liking anything better than ballet. I kept on worrying and worrying about what would happen if the Sheridan Academy didn't take me, and I didn't like thinking about it at all. I felt as though I had a big black hole in the middle of my mind, which I didn't dare look into. Every time I started wondering about it, I quickly made myself imagine something else, something really lovely, like whether I might be in this year's production of *The Nutcracker*.

"Here we are!" said Phoebe's mum, and we all stared out of the car in silence. The Sheridan Academy was a huge white house with pillars at the front. It was in a very quiet street, with trees growing all along the pavement.

"Posh, isn't it?" said Tony. Phoebe and I didn't say a thing. I don't know how Phoebe was feeling, but I had a really fluttery feeling in my stomach.

"I'm nervous," said Phoebe. "I don't know if we—"

"Nonsense!" I smiled at her. "We're just as good as anyone else from any other ballet school. We'll show them!"

"Honestly, Weezer, I don't know how you can be so calm," said Phoebe. She must have been feeling as nervous as I was, because she was usually very good about not calling me Weezer. But I was so pleased that she thought I was calm that I forgave her.

"I'm nervous too," I whispered. "But I'm not going to show it. Come on."

We opened the huge black door and the hall just inside was all marbled and echoey. A nice lady at a desk took our names and told us to go up the stairs to the cloakroom to change, and then into the waiting area.

"Everyone who's come for the audition," the lady told us, "will have a class together at ten o'clock, and then you'll be seen one at a time. Make sure you have your music tapes ready to take in with you when you're called for your interview with Madame Blanche."

Even though we tried to walk softly, our feet made a loud noise on the stone steps as we walked up. We could hear voices coming from behind a door, and Tony went ahead of us and pushed it open.

Chapter Five

"I never realised there'd be so many people," Tony whispered to me as we went into the cloakroom. There were about fifteen children getting ready, and putting on their ballet shoes, and crowding round the mirror at the far end of the room.

"We must be a bit late," I said. "Come on, let's hurry to get changed."

My heart was banging so hard in my chest by the time we were called that I didn't notice where we were taken, but soon we were in the most enormous room I'd ever seen, and right down at the other end there was an old lady with her hair in a tight bun, sitting on a chair with a very high back. She was wearing a black dress and a necklace made of great big yellow beads, which hung down to her knees.

She looked as old as Mrs Posnansky.

"Is she going to take the class?" I asked Phoebe. "I'm sure she must have been a dancer when she was young, don't you think?"

"Oh, yes," said Phoebe, "and I expect she's foreign too. Maybe she's Russian."

"No whispering, please," said a young man, who looked really nice. "The class is about to begin. My name is Miles. Take up your positions at the barre, please."

As soon as the class started, I forgot all about auditioning. I just listened to the lovely music coming from the piano, and made sure that my toes were pointed and that my arms were in the right places. At first I was worried in case we had to do things that Miss Matting hadn't taught us, but I soon saw that everything was almost the same: pliés, demi-pliés, entrechats, and port de bras. Miles was very kind and didn't shout. I worked harder at all my steps than I ever had, and I didn't even look round once to see how everyone else was doing. The class went by very quickly.

"Thank you, children," said Miles. "You've all done very well. Now if you go and wait in the room next to this one, we'll talk to you one at a time."

At first, it was quite fun, sitting in the waiting room. Tony and Phoebe and I discussed everyone else, but very quietly of course because we didn't want them to know we were talking about them.

"That girl in the pink leotard is lovely, isn't she?" said Phoebe.

"She might be too tall, don't you think?" said Tony.

"No, she's just right," I had to admit.

We did that for most of the others who were there, but in the end there was nothing else to say and we just had to wait to be called. After the class, everyone had scrabbled about in their bags to find their tapes with music for their solo dances, so I sat there turning mine over and over in my hands. I was called in quite near the beginning because my surname is Blair. Miles was waiting by the door to take me down to where the old lady was sitting.

"Louisa Blair, is that right?" he said. "Come and have a word with Madame Blanche."

The floor seemed to go on for ever. I tried to walk as daintily and gracefully as I could because I knew everyone was watching me. As well as Madame Blanche, there were three other people sitting at a table, with paper and pens in front of them. I knew they were all ready to write down things about my dancing, and how I answered questions.

"Good morning," said Madame Blanche, without smiling. "Why do you wish to come to the Sheridan Academy?"

I didn't know if there was a right answer to the question, so I just told the truth.

"My teacher, Miss Matting, is going away,

and everyone says Sheridan is the best ballet school in town. I couldn't bear not to go to ballet every week. I am going to be a ballerina when I grow up. I'm determined. I'm going to work very hard."

"Many little girls want to be ballerinas but very few succeed, do you know this?"

I nodded. "Yes, I do. But I still want to try. I think I could do it. I think I'm good enough."

As soon as the words were out of my mouth, I wished I hadn't said them. Madame Blanche would think I was so conceited. She wouldn't want such a boastful person in her school. I blushed and looked at my feet.

"Have you prepared a short dance for us?" she said.

"Yes," I answered. "It's a dance to some music from *Sleeping Beauty.*

"Have you got a tape, Louisa?" Miles asked. I gave him the tape I'd brought with me. He smiled at me and said, "Thank you . . . I'll just pop it into the machine . . . here we go."

The hall filled with the lovely sound of Tchaikovsky's music and at once I forgot all about Madame Blanche, and whether I'd spoiled everything for myself. I just began to dance as I'd danced to welcome Mrs Posnansky home, and everything faded away except the music and the movements I was making. At the end, I went to sit down again. The people with the paper in front of them had written things all over it.

"Thank you very much, my dear," said Madame Blanche, and she smiled at me. "You'll be hearing from us very soon."

Chapter Six

"I don't think," I said to Annie, "that people should say 'very soon' when they really mean ages and ages and ages. It's been more than a week now since the audition. When d'you think we're going to hear?"

Annie sighed. "You are a mega-pain in the neck, Weezer," she said. "You've been talking about nothing else for a whole week, and getting up early and waiting for the postman and generally making life miserable for yourself."

"I'm NOT called Weezer," I shouted back, as crossly as I could.

"I know you're not. I'm just trying to get you angry about something different, that's all. If you're yelling at me, you won't be fretting about getting a letter from the

Sheridan Academy."

"It won't come today now," I said. "I went out and spoke to Postie and made him look in the very bottom of his bag in case the letter had fallen out of a pile or something. And anyway, nothing ever comes on a Saturday, does it?"

Before Annie had time to answer, Mum called out from the hall.

"Telephone, Louisa. It's Phoebe." I went running downstairs as fast as I could and took the phone from Mum.

"Hello, Phoebe," I said. "What are you ringing about?"

"I've had a letter," said Phoebe. "From the Sheridan Academy. I've got in! They've offered me a place starting next term. Have you heard anything yet? Has the postman been?"

My mouth was suddenly dry and I closed my eyes because I thought I was going to faint. All sorts of things went through my mind and I just wanted to scream at Phoebe and say something like *How come you've got in and I haven't heard yet? I'm just as good a dancer as you are. I know I am . . . I just know it . . .* but I stopped myself in time and bit my lip to make sure I wouldn't cry on the phone.

"That's brilliant, Phoebe," I said. "I'm dead pleased for you. Really. Our post hasn't come yet."

Later on, I would think of something I could say to her, but now I couldn't bear to stay on the line for one moment longer, so I said, "Mum's waiting for me, Phoebe, so I've got to go. We're off to town in a minute. I'll ring you later. Bye!"

I almost threw the phone down on the hall table and ran back upstairs to our

bedroom, flung myself on to the bed and started to howl into my pillow.

"Louisa?" Annie came to sit next to me, and she touched me on the shoulder. "I bet I know what she said, right? She's got in, hasn't she?"

I turned round and went right on howling.

"Why haven't I got in, Annie? It's not fair! I'm as good as Phoebe, I am really. Why haven't I been chosen?" I sobbed and sobbed and nothing Annie could say made any difference.

"You should phone Tony," she said at last and I sat up and wiped my nose and eyes with a tissue that she was holding out to me.

"If *he's* got in and I haven't . . ." I began, but Annie said:

"Just go and speak to him. You have to calm down a bit. You can't go on crying for ever."

Annie was wrong. I'm sure I *could* have gone on crying for ever, but I thought I'd start after I'd spoken to Tony. I dialled his number and waited for him to answer. When he did I said, "Phoebe's got into the Sheridan Academy. She phoned me a bit ago. Have you heard anything?"

"Yeah," Tony said calmly.

"Are you going to tell me if you've got in or what?" I shrieked at him.

"Give me a chance! I haven't got in. I don't

care, though."

"Bet you do. Bet you care and you're just not saying."

"Well, it would have been good to get in, but I did tell you, Weezer, that I wanted to do gym instead. Don't you remember?"

The tears were pouring down my cheeks again. I couldn't help it. I said, "My name's not Weezer!" and turned the phone off before he could say another word.

Chapter Seven

How could Tony be so calm about everything? I sat down on the floor next to Bradman, our cat, who was stretched out on the doormat fast asleep and not caring at all that I was so miserable. I was still holding my tissue and it was all soggy and disgusting. Just then, there was a knock at the door. I ran upstairs at once. I didn't want anyone to see me with horrible red eyes, especially not Tony. I was almost sure that it was him at the door, because he really doesn't like it when I shout at him, and this time I'd really screamed. Poor Tony! I hid on the landing while Mum opened the door, peering through the banisters and down into the hall. It wasn't Tony. It was Mrs Posnansky.

I ran downstairs again, still crying. I wanted to tell Mrs Posnansky the bad news at once, about Phoebe getting in and me not even getting a letter. She would know how to cheer me up.

Mum said, "Louisa, just let Mrs Posnansky sit down and get comfortable before you tell her all your troubles."

We went into the kitchen. Just at that moment, I didn't feel like being nice to Mrs Posnansky and letting her sit down. I wanted everyone to cheer *me* up. Why didn't they realise how miserable I was feeling? Couldn't they see that I'd been crying?

Mrs Posnansky walked very slowly, and once she was sitting down at the table, she said, "I come straight away. There is letter here for Louisa. That postman, he left it for me. It is mistake. It is my house number, but the name is not me. The name is: *Miss Louisa Blair.*"

I was trembling all over. I looked at the envelope in Mrs Posnansky's hand and even upside down I could see the Sheridan Academy logo in the corner: a pair of ballet shoes with their ribbons crossed, in pale blue. I couldn't help myself. I went right up to Mrs Posnansky and took the envelope from her hand.

"That's it," I whispered. "That's the letter from the Sheridan Academy, isn't it?" I could feel myself trembling. "I don't want to open it. I don't dare. You do it, Annie."

"Are you sure?"

I nodded and gave her the envelope and closed my eyes while she tore it open. All sorts of thoughts were whirling round in my head, making me feel dizzy. I'd been accepted . . . they didn't want me. No, they did . . . they didn't. I couldn't bear it.

"You've got in, Weezer! You really have. Look! Look what it says . . ."

I grabbed the page out of her hand and there they were: the words I'd been so, so longing to see: *We are happy to inform you . . .*

"They're happy to inform me! I'm happy! I'm so happy . . . I must phone Phoebe . . . oh, isn't it marvellous? I'm going to the Sheridan Academy too! I'm going to be a ballerina. Mrs Posnansky, isn't it wonderful?"

I started dancing round and round the kitchen. Mum said, "That's great, Louisa, but we do have to discuss the matter of fees, you know. It *is* rather a lot of money. We'll have to talk to your father."

I couldn't believe it. Did she mean that I wasn't going to be able to go to the Sheridan Academy, even now that I'd got in? That would have been worse than terrible. I was just going to open my mouth to say so, when Mrs Posnansky said,

"Forgive me, Louisa, darling, but I think of this, since audition. I know from your mama how much is the fee they ask for the lessons, and so I think, I would like to spend the money that is mine on Louisa, to make her a ballet dancer. If I leave you my money when I die, it will be too late. Now is when you need what I can give, and so I decide I pay for my darling Little Swan to be trained for the ballet. It is pleasure for me."

I didn't know what to say. I looked at Mum who was smiling and at Annie who was bright red in the face and at Mrs Posnansky who was the kindest person in the whole world.

"You're like my Fairy Godmother," I said, and I ran to hug her. "Thank you! When I'm a ballerina I'll tell everyone it's because you helped me when I was a little girl."

"Then I will be famous, together with you!" she said. "I will share your dancing. This is very good. I am most happy!"

"And I'm happy too!" I said. "I'm going to work so hard. You'll be proud of me, you'll see."

"Already now, I am proud," Mrs Posnansky said. She had tears in her eyes. She always cried when she was happy.

"I'll make us all a cup of coffee," Mum said, "and we must have some cake to celebrate."

"I'm just going to phone Phoebe and tell her," I said.

I pointed my toes as I walked into the

hall, and raised my arms above my head, and looked at myself in the mirror by the front door. I really *was* going to be a proper ballet dancer. I smiled at my reflection and started to dial Phoebe's number.

RED FOX BALLET BOOKS

Little Swan

Louisa's Secret

Louisa in the Wings

A Rival for Louisa

Louisa on Screen